SANDY HOLLOW

J.S. CUNCLE

SPRING FORTH
PUBLISHING

SANDY HOLLOW

This story is a work of fiction. Any names, characters, places, and incidents are the product of the authors imagination. Any resemblance to persons, living or dead, is entirely coincidental.

ISBN: 979-8-9888274-0-5 (paperback)

Cover Design by Jeremy Scheitzach

Published by Spring Forth Publishing LLC

For my family.
Thank you for your love and support.

CONTENTS

Chapter 1

A Nice Little Town

The relentless rain pounds on the windshield of the little 1967 VW Beetle, as the wipers work tirelessly in an attempt to provide a clear view for the driver. In the driver's seat, seventeen-year-old Maggie Billings keeps a white-knuckle grip on the steering wheel as she navigates the winding, mountain road; squinting to read the road signs between the lightning flashes and the glare from the oncoming headlights. She feathers the gas pedal as the engine emits a horrible screeching noise and the headlights dim slightly as the tired, little bug has been doing off and on for the last several miles.

"Come on baby," she pleads as she tries to will the car to keep running. "Just a couple more miles. You can do it."

She feels a sense of relief as she passes a wooden sign that reads, "Welcome to Sandy Hollow." She can make out the outlines of a few of the small buildings as she tries to identify a mechanics garage to pull into.

As it happens, Sandy Hollow is Maggie's destination, where she is supposed to meet up with her father and brother at her Uncle Jake's cabin, where he has lived in the tiny town since before she was born. This was to be a fun-filled, spring-break fishing trip but so far, the weather doesn't seem to be cooperating on the first day. Maggie's mother was unable to take time off work to join them and she had strong reservations about letting their young daughter drive up alone. Her dad, however, advocated for her, pointing out that she is almost eighteen and very responsible, and her mom eventually agreed, although reluctantly, to let her go. Now Maggie just hopes she can make it to the garage where she can call her dad to come pick her up.

Up ahead she can see an old, run-down looking building with two big garage doors and a sign that reads, "Dale's Automotive." She starts to turn in until she notices the "closed" sign hanging on the door and can see that there are no lights on inside the shop. She turns the car back onto the road and keeps driving, slowly, as she searches for another place to stop. The car squeals in protest as the headlights dim again. Maggie strains to see through the rain-soaked windshield until she notices a small diner up ahead with a few cars parked out front. She can make out the name, "Molly's" over the front porch and decides that's her best bet for getting help.

Maggie just manages to maneuver the car into a parking spot out front before it sputters and finally dies. *Good timing*, she thinks to herself as she sighs and rests her forehead on the steering wheel, allowing her tensed body to finally relax. She only allows herself a moment before she sits up and takes her phone from her purse in the passenger seat next to her. She taps her dad's number from the dropdown menu, but the screen flashes "no service."

"Oh, you've got to be kidding me!" she exclaims, as she waves the phone around the interior of the car in a futile attempt to detect a signal within the small space.

Well, maybe there's a phone I can use inside, she thinks to herself as she drops the phone back into her purse and adjusts the rear-view mirror to check her hair and makeup. She runs her fingers through her thick, blonde hair as it softly falls just over her shoulders. Maggie is a very pretty girl, though she deals with the typical self-image issues that most teenage girls do. Even though she is very slender, she always seems to find a little spot around her waist, or under her chin that she wishes were a bit thinner, or tighter; not to mention her cheekbones and lips which she's always felt could be better. Then there's her brown eyes, which she's always wished were the beautiful green color of her mother's. Instead, she's had to

3

learn to live with her father's dark brown eyes. *"Well, it is what it is,"* she always tells herself, as she does now while pushing the mirror back and grabbing her purse as she makes a dash for the diner through the pouring rain.

Maggie bursts through the front door to the jingling of bells that hang from the knob, slightly surprising the people inside. She stands there for a moment as she takes in the sight of the quaint little establishment. To the right are several empty booths and tables with a soft, crackling fire burning in a stone fireplace along the wall, while to the left, a few people sit in some of the four booths along the front windows, and at the counter. A sweet, motherly looking woman, with grayish-blonde hair, appearing to be in her late fifties, or early sixties stands behind the counter. Maggie notices a name tag on her apron with the name Molly and figures she must be the owner.

"Well, bless your heart sweetie, come in out of that rain," she says, waiving her hand in a beaconing motion. She pats the counter in front of one of the empty bar stools. "You come sit yourself down right here and get warm."

Maggie slowly makes her way to the counter as she looks around at the other people in the room. In the first booth next to the door are two young men, both slender in build, but strong looking, appearing to be in their early twenties and both slightly dirty looking. The first man has on a dingy looking trucker cap and has some black grease under his fingernails, while the other looks to be slightly cleaner, but with a head of matted hair, suggesting that he was wearing a hat, but must have removed it before sitting down. In the next both is a feeble-looking, elderly woman with a somewhat odd expression, as she stares at Maggie while rocking back and forth slightly in her seat. At the counter, a weathered, middle-aged look-ing woman with a dark brown braid hanging down her back sits in the middle seat finishing what looks to have been a chicken-fried steak and coffee. Mag-gie thinks she looks to be some kind of rancher maybe. Finally, at the end of the counter against the wall, a large strong-looking man with just a little ex-tra weight in the mid-section sits wearing a big cow-boy hat, hunched over a piece of apple pie, which seems to demand his full attention.

Maggie sets her purse on the counter as she slides up onto the tall stool.

"My car broke down out front and I can't seem to get a cell signal to call my dad," she begins. "I tried to stop at the garage down the street, but it's closed."

The woman behind the counter looks to the man in the trucker hat, "Brian, do you know where Dale is?"

"He's stayin' with his cousin, Tom, up in Aspen Cove," the man says as he stands up from the booth. "He said he won't be back for a couple of days." He takes a step closer to Maggie as he puts his thumbs through his belt loops. "What kinda trouble you havin' with your car there, Miss?"

"Well, a few miles down the road it started making a loud screeching noise and the headlights would dim when it did."

Brian rubs his chin thoughtfully. "Huh, well that sounds like it might be the alternator, but I can't be sure unless I take a look at it."

"Well?" the woman behind the counter says with a shrug. "Go look at it, Brian. Don't just stand there holdin' the floor down."

"But Molly," Brian says gesturing toward the window, "it's stormin' pretty good out there."

"Well, that's what your raincoat's for, Sugar," she says pointing toward the coatrack.

Brian turns and grabs a yellow raincoat from the rack. He grumbles something under his breath as he puts it on and starts to open the door.

"Aren't you forgetting something?" Molly points to the keys on the counter. "You might want to take the keys with you."

Maggie grabs the keys and turns to hand them to the sulking young man.

"Thanks for taking a look at it," she says as she places the keys into his open palm.

"Well, guess I don't have nothin' better to do," he says as he takes them. "I'll be back in a minute," he grumbles as he turns and heads out into the stormy weather.

"Don't worry," Molly says with a smile. "A little water will do him good. Now, can I get you something to eat while you're waiting? Sam's just about the best cook around these parts and he can fix you up somethin' right quick."

Maggie peers through the narrow passthrough window behind the counter and sees a sweaty, overweight man she hadn't noticed before, standing over a grill, apparently trying to clean it. He looks up from his work just long enough to nod to her and then returns his attention to the greasy surface again.

"Oh, no thanks," Maggie says as she takes her phone from her purse. "I was trying to call my dad, but I can't seem to get a signal."

"That's 'cause there ain't no cell towers 'round these parts," says the lady sitting at the counter as she finishes the last bite of her meal, wipes her mouth with her napkin and crumples it up before throwing it on her plate. "You gotta go about two towns over to get a signal for one of those things."

"Is your dad staying around these parts?" Molly asks as she picks up the woman's plate and sets it down behind the counter.

"Yeah," Maggie replies. "He and my brother are staying with my Uncle Jake. I'm supposed to meet up with them today."

"Oh my gosh!" Molly exclaims, leaning back a little and showing an expression of surprise. "You're Jake's niece, 'little Magpie.'"

Maggie is surprised to hear the woman use that name, as it is a nickname used almost exclusively by her family. "Uh, yeah. Have we met before?"

"Oh, it's been a long time. I'm sure you don't remember; you were pretty young. I do know your uncle though. Of course, everybody knows everybody else in this little town."

"Well, that's great," Maggie says. "Do you know how I can get in touch with him so they can come get me?"

"Sure sweetie," Molly says as she takes a landline phone from behind the counter and sets it on top. "You can give 'em a call from here."

"Thanks," Maggie says as she puts the receiver to her ear. Before she can dial, she hears a soft crackling sound over the line instead of the expected dial tone. "Oh, I think there's something wrong with the line."

"Oh, let me see," Molly says as she takes the receiver to try and get a tone. She looks to the large man at the end of the counter. "Joe, do you know anything about the phone lines being down?"

"Mm-hmm," the man grunts while still leaning over his plate as he scrapes up the last of the apple pie he's been devouring in a manner resembling a grizzly bear trying to protect his food as he eats. "Sarah said we could expect some power failures and downed phone lines with the storm."

Maggie hadn't looked very closely before, but now notices the gun on the man's belt and the sheriff's star pinned to his dark brown shirt. He gulps down the last of his coffee and stands up, pulling his pants and gun-belt up as he walks over.

"Incidentally, I spoke with Jake this morning," he says, "and the three of them were driving down to Logger's Creek to see about borrowing Doc Peterson's boat. I expect there gonna have to hold up there for the night. Turns out the river's been rising and the bridge was closed not long after they left."

"Oh no," Molly exclaims. "Do you need a place to stay, Hun? I've got an extra room upstairs if you want."

"Oh, thanks, but that's ok. I think I'll just go to my uncle's cabin. My dad gave me a key." She looks back to the sheriff. "Can you tell me how to get there from here?"

"It's not too far," the sheriff says, pointing out the window. "It's just a little way up the hill there, but the road's a dirt road. Might be a little too muddy for your bug out there."

Just then, Brian comes bursting in through the door, dripping wet as he takes his raincoat off and hangs it back on the hook. "Well, I got some good news and some bad news," he says as he walks over. "The good news is your alternator's fine. The bad news is your belt's shot and it looks like you need a new pully nut. Them old Volkswagens got kind of a funny belt tension system compared to most other cars."

"Oh, see?" Molly says, looking concerned. "I really think you oughta stay here tonight."

Maggie looks to the sheriff. "Would you be able to drive me up there?"

"Well, I really need to go check on some of the lower properties with the rising river water," he says, rubbing the back of his neck. "Gotta make sure nobody's getting into trouble now that the storm's pickin' up."

"Brian, you could drive her up to Jake's place," Molly says.

"Yeah, I got the wrecker out there. I can take you up there if you want," he says with a slight smile that normally could have made Maggie feel a bit uncomfortable, though she doesn't think about it now as she's more focused on getting to the cabin.

"Sure, I'd really appreciate it," she says, standing up from her seat. "I'll just grab my bag out of my car."

"Ain't a good idea," the little old lady says, causing everyone to fall silent and turn to look at her. She continues to slowly rock back and forth as she looks up at Maggie with an unsettling smile that causes a shiver to run up her spine. "Ain't safe for pretty young girls in these woods," she says and then gives a very soft, cackling laugh.

"Momma!" Molly says, putting her hands on the counter and leaning forward toward the old lady.

"She looks like all them others," she continues, still maintaining her eye lock with Maggie. "She's gonna end up like all them others."

"Momma that's enough!" Molly says firmly as she makes her way around the counter, walking over to sit down next to the old woman in an attempt to quiet her down.

Maggie is stunned as she feels a tight, queasy feeling in her stomach. "I think I better get going," she says softly, still looking at the woman.

"I'll start the truck," Brian says, grabbing his coat from the hook. Everyone else starts to shake off the event too as they all express needing to get going as well.

"Yeah, I better get a move on," the sheriff says as he opens the door and holds it for Maggie. She slowly makes her way to exit the dinner as he looks at her and says in a soft, reassuring tone, "Don't you pay no mind to that, young lady. Sandy Hollow is a real nice little town."

"Thanks," Maggie says in a quiet, troubled manner as she moves past the large man and into the storm outside.

Chapter 2

The Cabin

Maggie sits quietly in the front passenger seat of the truck, still troubled by what the old lady had said back at the diner. She can't help but wonder what she meant about the "others." It seemed obvious that there was something wrong with her mentally, but there was something about the way she had looked into her eyes that was still gnawing at her.

She looks over at Brian who is trying to keep the lumbering, old truck on the muddy roadway. He grumbles and swears under his breath as he navigates the steep incline, adjusting the wipers to their highest setting as the tires slip back and forth and the engine revs and groans. Maggie keeps trying to bring herself to ask him about the old lady, but can't seem to figure out how to begin.

"Come on!" Brian yells as the tires spin and the vehicle slides and rocks. He looks over at Maggie to see her staring at him with a distressed expression on her face. "Sorry there, Miss," he says. "I didn't mean to upset ya."

"Oh no," Maggie responds quickly. "That's not why I…" She searches for the right words. "I mean, I…"

"Oh, I see," Brian says, nodding his head as he focuses back on the road. "You're still thinkin' 'bout what old Mrs. Baker said back at Molly's."

"Well, yeah," Maggie says with a sense of relief that they are finally talking about it. "I mean, what *was* that?"

"Oh, ya know," he begins. "That's just Molly's mom, old Mrs. Baker. She ain't all there, if ya know what I mean."

"You mean she's crazy?" Maggie asks.

"Well, some think so, on account of her grandson, Danny; but the Doc says she's got that Alzheimer condition or somethin'."

"What about her grandson?"

"Danny Baker, he was Molly Baker's boy. He died a long time ago, kinda sudden like, under what some consider 'mysterious circumstances.'"

"'*Mysterious?*'"

"Yeah, well the story goes he was so upset about somthin' that happened where he and some girl he was in love with got stranded out in the woods somewhere. I guess she ended up dying and he made it back to town only to end up drownin' in the river about a week or so later."

"That's awful!"

"Yeah," Brian continues. "I guess he was supposed to be really good around water and swimmin' and stuff, which is why some people suspect he committed suicide, on account of his grief and all. After that, Mrs. Baker started acting more and more peculiar which is why some think she just went crazy, but others say she's just sick in the head with that Alzheimer stuff."

"When did this all happen?"

"Not real sure. I think it was about fifteen or maybe twenty years ago; or somewhere abouts."

"Do you know what she meant by the 'others?'"

"What?" Brian asks with a quick glance in Maggie's direction.

"She said I look like all the others, and that I would end up like all the others."

"Oh yeah," Brian says, keeping his eyes on the road, but looking a little uncomfortable with the question. "Well, ya know, there's a lot of them urban legends 'round these parts. Things about young girls goin' missing and all."

"Is there any truth to the legends?" Maggie asks, feeling a shiver as she realizes she might not want to hear the answer.

"Well, I suppose I might remember some things about some young girls a couple years back that got lost or something. Some think it might be tied to Danny's story and all."

"How so?"

"Well I hear the girlfriend was a young blond girl, ya know, real pretty and all." He looks over at Maggie. "Probably about your age I guess."

Maggie suddenly feels very uncomfortable.

"Anyway, there's always been a lot of crazy talk about stuff like serial killers, and ghosts and stuff like that." He gives a little chuckle. "That ain't even the craziest though. Some stories talk about everything from space aliens to even that bigfoot fella."

Suddenly, Brian slams on the breaks and the truck slides to a stop just before running into a large tree laying across the road.

"Whoa!" Brian exclaims. "Looks like that big, rotten tree finally gave up."

Maggie can see a porch light up ahead through the wind, rain and trees.

"Is that my uncle's cabin up ahead there?"

"Yeah," Brian answers. "That's Jake's place, but I don't think we're gonna be able to get around this giant tumble weed here."

Maggie looks at the tree and the light and determines she can make it the rest of the way on foot.

"That's alright," she says as she grabs her bag and starts to reach for the door handle. "I think I'll be fine from here."

"You sure about that?" Brian says, causing Maggie to pause. A crooked smile creeps across his face as he leans closer and puts his arm along the back of the seat, resting his hand just behind Maggie's head. The gesture makes her feel uneasy and causes her to shrink away. "You know, it might not be the best idea for you to stay there all alone. Why don't you let me take you back to town? You can stay at my place if you want."

"Thanks, but no thanks," Maggie says as she opens the door with a cold blast. "I'm perfectly capable of taking care of myself." She steps out onto the muddy ground and shuts the door before Brian can respond. She hops up and over the large tree laying across the road and looks back to see Brian looking at her from inside the truck, still smiling. He waves to her as she turns and starts up the hill toward the cabin.

The cold rain stings her face as she works to keep her footing in the slick mud. She starts to feel a little out of breath and thinks it must be partly due to the higher elevation, as she is in good physical condition. She's always been athletic, competing in basketball, track and swimming.

She makes it to the L-shaped, covered porch that wraps around the front and side of the old cabin. As she reaches the top of the front steps, she turns to see Brian turning the truck around and starting back down the hill. Feeling a sense of relief at seeing him leave, she takes a key from her pocket and moves to open the front door. After fumbling with the lock for a bit, the door creaks open and she enters the cabin where she quickly drops her bag and shuts and locks the door behind her.

The wind and rain assault the exterior of the cabin and Maggie can hear some of the many items hanging on the walls outside rattling and pounding against the house. She looks around the dim interior and moves to an old table lamp, turning it on to provide some much welcome light to the place. She looks about again and feels a sense of nostalgic familiarity with the old cabin, even though she hasn't been there since she was very young.

The design of the cabin is simple. Standing with her back to the door, she can see the living room area to her left, with a couch, chair, and a stone fireplace in the middle of the left wall. Two large windows flank both sides of the fireplace and provide an open view of the side porch and the woods beyond. To her right is the kitchen, with an L-shaped counter, containing a sink and stove along the right wall. A small window sits over the sink and a door to the left of the counter leads to the outside. An old, oak table with four chairs sits in the middle of the kitchen area and directly in front of her is a staircase that leads to the bedrooms upstairs.

Maggie removes her rain-soaked jacket and hangs it on a hook next to the front door to dry. She kneels down and removes a towel from her bag to dry her hair. She wraps the towel around her head as she moves to the phone on a small table in the living room. She picks up the receiver and hears the same crackling static she heard at the diner.

"Still no phone," she says to herself as she hangs up. She looks up the stairs where she can see a soft glow of light. "Let's have a quick look around," she says as she slowly moves to the stairs. She speaks out loud to herself because she feels a little uneasy and somehow it helps her not to feel so alone. She notices a rugged walking stick leaning against the wall at the base of the steps and decides to take it with her. She removes the damp towel from her head and drapes it over the wooden knob at the bottom of the rail as she reaches for the stick.

Maggie cautiously searches all the rooms upstairs and when she is satisfied that she is truly alone, she returns downstairs and puts the stick back in its place. The wind continues to disturb the items hanging on the outside walls, causing a soft, rhythmic thumping. She looks at the fireplace and then back at a tea pot in the kitchen.

"That's what I need," she says. "A nice fire and a cup of hot tea is just what the doctor ordered." She thinks for a moment, then walks to the kitchen. "Tea first."

As she takes the tea pot and starts rinsing it out, the thumping on the wall grows louder. She tries to ignore it as she fills the pot and places it on the stovetop. She turns the heat on as there is a sudden loud crashing sound which causes her to jump and spin around. Through one of the windows in the living room she can see a large shadowy figure standing on the porch, backlit by a flash of lightning. It looks to be someone standing there looking at her through the window with two outstretched arms. She feels a sudden rush of sheer terror rise up inside of her as one of the panes of glass breaks, causing her to involuntarily let out a bloodcurdling scream.

Chapter 3

From The Shadows

Maggie stands silently in the kitchen, paralyzed with fear. She stares, wide-eyed at the large figure that still menacingly fills the window frame, staring back at her from the darkness, unmoving as the wind whistles and howls through the pane of broken glass. Her mind fights through an adrenaline induced fog as she tries to reason through the situation. *What should I do? Should I run? Should I fight? Can I fight him? Who is he? What does he want? Why hasn't he moved, or tried to come inside?*

She feels herself coming back to her senses as she cautiously takes a step forward. Another flash of lightning illuminates her tormentor from behind, again revealing the bulk of his mass. He still hasn't moved.

Maggie takes a few quick steps over to the walking stick leaning against the wall at the base of the stairs. She grabs the stick and clutches it close to her body, defensively, as she waits to see if her movements will provoke any reaction. The figure remains unchanged.

With the stick held out in front of her, she slowly and carefully makes her way to the window. Each step causes the old, wooden floorboards to creak and crack under her feet. The wind moans and howls through the broken glass, as if warning her to stay away. As she gets close to the window, she can't help noticing that there seems to be something strange about the shape of the figure. She reaches over and turns on a lamp that is next to the window. The light reveals the object outside to be a large, stuffed moose head.

"Oh, you're kidding me!" she exclaims aloud as she lowers the stick and relaxes her tensed muscles. "It's only Norman."

Norman is the old moose her uncle has had hanging out on his porch since before Maggie was born. When they were kids, she and her brother took it upon themselves to name him. Her brother wanted to name him Bullwinkle after the cartoon, but Maggie insisted he looked like a Norman. Now that she is older, she has no idea what her reasoning was, but everyone thought it was cute at the time, and from that point on he was known as Norman the moose.

Maggie now feels a sense of embarrassment for her reaction to what turned out to be a stuffed moose head. "Sure glad no one was here to witness that little, hysterical episode," she says to herself. "Get a grip Maggie!"

She stands there trying to think as a cold blast of air rushes through the broken pane, causing her to shiver. "I'm gonna have to do something about that," she says to herself. She looks around for a small piece of wood, cardboard, or anything she can use to cover the opening. She walks through the kitchen, opening drawers in her search. She finds a little cutting board but decides it would be too heavy to attach to the window.

As she stands there running her hand through her hair, she sees the closed door leading to the pantry near the stairs. She opens it and steps inside, feeling for the pull chain on the lightbulb that hangs from the ceiling. When she locates it, she gives it a pull, bathing the small room in light. The pantry walls are lined with wooden shelves, containing food, tools and other various items. She finds a stack of disposable, plastic plates and picks one up to examine it. "This'll work," she says to herself as she looks around for some tape.

As she visually scans the shelves, her gaze moves upward where she spies a roll of grey duct tape on the top shelf. She steps forward and strains to reach it as the floor creaks and bends slightly beneath her feet. She takes the roll of tape from its perch and steps back as she looks down to inspect the floor. When she sees what she was standing on, she feels a chill of fear creep over her, causing the hair on the back of her neck to stand and goosebumps to raise on her arms. It is an old feeling of fear; something from long ago, when she was a child, that has returned to her, like the memory of a dream one tries to bury in the back of their mind.

Maggie is frozen for an instant as she looks at a square door on the floor of the pantry. The door is made of the same boards as the rest of the floor, with a tarnished, brass ring attached to one side. If lifted, the door reveals a ladder that goes down to a dark cellar beneath the cabin.

The reason for Maggie's reaction again goes back to when she and her brother were children. Her brother had terrified her with a story of a small creature that lived in the cellar beneath the house. He said the creature was like a troll, like those they spoke of in fairy tales that would wait beneath bridges for unsuspecting travelers to pass by. In fact, he had convinced her that the fairy tales were based on the very creature living down there, as he was very old. He told her that he usually slept, but occasionally had to sneak out to hunt and feed; and while his diet normally consisted of various animals, occasionally he took small children.

The story had terrified her to the point of once even causing her to stay awake all night, crying quietly in the darkness. She had considered telling her parents about what her brother had told her, but he convinced her that it would do no good, as adults are not capable of seeing the creature and therefore could not believe in him.

As Maggie grew older, she realized that the story wasn't true and was just another mean trick her brother had played on her. He always seemed to delight in teasing her, as most siblings do. Nevertheless, the sight of the cellar door had brought back, if only for a moment, that feeling of terror that once consumed her as a child.

Maggie relaxes again as she stands outside the pantry, still staring at the cellar door on the floor. She lets out a sigh as she sets the plate and tape on the kitchen table. The calm is again broken as her heart leaps and she spins around with a gasp at the sound of a high-pitched squeal coming from the tea pot.

"Enough already," she yells as she rushes over to remove the pot from the heat. She turns the knob off on the stove and turns to the empty house to vent her frustration. "I'm sick of this! I hate this place! I hate this storm! I hate that creepy, old lady from the diner! I hate that moose! I hate that door! I want to go home! I want to go back to civilization, and normal people, and get out of this Twilight Zone version of Mayberry!"

Her rant is answered only by the sound of the wind, howling through the broken glass and the rain pounding against the cabin's exterior. She turns and takes a cup from the cabinet behind her and drops a tea bag in. She pours the steaming hot liquid from the pot into the cup and leaves it sitting on the counter to brew as she goes about trying to fix the window.

Maggie tries to cover the broken pane with the plastic plate, but the piece of the moose antler protruding through prevents her from doing so effectively. She tries to push the antler back through, taking care not to cut herself on the jagged glass. After several failed attempts, she stands up straight and comes to the conclusion, "I have to go outside."

The thought of having to venture out into the stormy darkness does not appeal to her, but Maggie knows that she must if she is to stop the wind from coming through. She walks over to the front door and puts her jacket and shoes on. They are still a bit damp from her earlier dash to the cabin. She unlocks and opens the door and is greeted by a blast of cold, damp wind.

Maggie holds her jacket closed as she runs out onto the porch and rounds the corner to the broken window. She sees the moose head resting on an old, wooden table in front of the window. She tugs on the moose, trying to dislodge the antler from the window. It taps against the frame, causing her to stop for fear of breaking more glass. She then grabs hold of the edge of the table and gently slides it back, bring-ing the head and antler with it, away from the win-dow.

She stands there assessing her work and sees that the antler is now clear of the glass. She is about to go back inside to tape the plate over the window when something out of the corner of her eye catches her attention. Some brief flash of movement that causes her to snap her eyes to the dark forest to see what lurks there. Her heart pounds and her eyes strain in the blackness, but she can only make out the shadows of the trees closest to her. A bright flash of lightning followed by a loud clap of thunder momentarily illu-minates the area, but Maggie cannot see anything that may have been responsible for the movement she thought she saw.

Staring into the darkness, she feels uneasy, as though something were watching her from the inky shadows. As though the forest itself were stalking her like some looming predator. She tries to shake off the feeling, reasoning that she's just on edge. *It's proba-bly just a frightened deer,* she thinks to herself. She pushes aside the thought that a deer wouldn't be run-ning around in the storm, and decides she had better hurry back inside.

Back in the house, Maggie goes to work taping the plate over the broken windowpane. When finished, she is pleased at how well it has functioned and stands to admire her handy work. Her gaze then shifts past the window's interior, to the dark forest beyond, where she thought she had seen something moving. A slight shutter envelopes her body, as she can't shake the persistent feeling that something, or someone is watching her.

Chapter 4

The Visitor

From the living room window, Maggie stares into the blackness of the forest, as if it were alive and staring back at her. A staring contest with a monster, waiting to devour her the moment she blinks. She glances up to see if there is a shade or blind to close, but sees only a dusty valance. She looks around the room at the other windows, feeling very exposed, but they are all the same. No curtains, blinds or shades on any of the downstairs windows; only valances.

"Wow, talk about living in a fishbowl," she says aloud. "I guess when you live this far out in the forest, you don't usually worry about people looking in your windows."

Another flash of lightning briefly illuminates the surrounding environment and is followed by a loud clap of thunder that causes the walls of the little, old cabin to tremble. At this point, Maggie's nerves are so strained, she can't help but feel as though the slight shaking of the walls is somehow a sympathetic reflection of her own fear and anxiety.

Maggie steps back and tries to refocus her thoughts. She then remembers the cup of tea on the kitchen counter. She walks over and removes the bag from the still steaming cup. Normally she would drink the tea straight, as she always makes an effort to reduce her caloric intake, but tonight she decides she needs a little comfort. She reaches for a sugar bowl that sits toward the back of the counter and drops in one heaping spoonful. She then makes her way over to the refrigerator where she finds a small carton of half-and-half. She pours a little into the dark, brown liquid and watches for a moment as the cream slowly swirls in the cup, mixing with the tea in a somewhat satisfyingly therapeutic dance. She returns the carton to the fridge and picks up the warm cup, holding it close to her body as she inhales the rising steam and allows the warmth to absorb into her hands.

This brief moment of serenity is a welcome change to the stressful events that have so mercilessly bombarded her thus far. She closes her eyes and tries to prolong the moment as much as possible.

With a soft sigh of contentment, Maggie slowly opens her eyes and decides to address her next to-do item and make a fire. She slowly makes her way over to the living room, takes a sip of her tea and sets the cup on a small table next to the chair. She then kneels down by the fireplace to inspect the flue, trying to remember what her father taught her about building a fire. Peering up the chimney and placing her hand inside, she can tell that the damper is closed. She looks to the front of the old, brick fireplace and sees the handle for the damper and adjusts it to the open position. She places her hand inside again and feels a draft of cold air coming down into the firebox. She remembers something her father had told her about warming the inside of the firebox by rolling a newspaper into a cone and burning it inside the box until the airflow reverses and travels up the chimney.

Maggie looks to the side of the fireplace and sees a stack of wood and an old, metal box filled with splinters of kindling. On the floor next to the box is a stack of old newspapers. Maggie takes some of the newspaper and crumples a few pieces up and gently sets it inside the fireplace. She grabs several pieces of kindling wood and arranges them like a small tee-pee over the paper. She then rolls a couple of pieces of the newspaper into a cone and looks around her for some matches. She spies a matchbox sitting on the mantel and grunts as she reaches for them from her kneeling position. She strikes a match and watches the little flame burst to life and dance on the end of the matchstick before holding it to light the end of the cone. Holding the burning paper inside the fireplace, the flame and smoke swirl and move erratically for a moment until the warmth causes the airflow to change and draw upwards into the chimney. She quickly holds the flame to the crumpled paper and kindling and watches as it takes hold and grows into a small fire, with the satisfying crackle and snaps of the dry kindling wood. She then takes a couple of small logs and positions them carefully over the blaze, watching to see if it catches to the logs. After a moment where the flames almost die down, they slowly start to rise again as the logs begin to burn. Within a few minutes, there is a nice warm fire burning within the fireplace.

Maggie places a larger log atop the other two and reaches for her tea cup, taking a sip as she settles back on the floor, sitting cross-legged in front of the fireplace. She holds the cup and stares, somewhat trance-like, at the hypnotic flames that gently dance and lick at the logs. The soothing heat feels good on her face and the quiet, crackling sounds are calming, even juxtaposed with the howling wind and pounding rains that rage just outside.

"What is it about fire," she says aloud, her gaze still fixed. It dawns on her that for the first time, since she arrived, her anxiety is finally beginning to melt away. She feels a great sense of appreciation for this much needed moment of calm, and she takes a slow, deep breath, trying to focus on the tranquility and prolong it as much as possible.

Maggie's focus is suddenly broken as another flash of lightning illuminates the world beyond the cabin and in her peripheral vision, she notices movement outside the window. She snaps her head toward the window and gasps to see two glowing eyes staring back at her. Her body tenses and she nearly drops the tea cup as yet another adrenaline surge jolts through her. The lightning flashes again and briefly reveals the outline of a small cat sitting on the table outside, peering at her through the glass.

"Oh my gosh," Maggie exclaims, jumping to her feet and setting the cup back on the table as she rushes to the window. The little cat stands and moves closer, obviously seeking help and shelter from the storm. Maggie turns and rushes for the front door. She quickly unlocks and opens it as she steps out and looks to the side.

"Here kitty, kitty," she calls in a sympathetic tone. The soggy, little feline comes running around the corner and doesn't even hesitate as it passes Maggie and stops just inside the door. Maggie closes the door and bends down to pick it up, holding it's cold, trembling, little body close to hers.

"Oh, you poor, little baby," she says as she walks over to the kitchen counter to pick up a towel lying on the surface. She wraps the towel around the cat as he begins to purr with her caring touch. She sets him on the table and begins drying him with the towel, trying to soak as much water as possible from his fur.

She sees that he is a little tuxedo cat, mostly charcoal grey with a white patch on his chest, like a white, dress shirt and a little patch on his chin that looks like a little milk beard. He also has white tips on all four paws.

"Well, aren't you a handsome little guy," she says, picking him up and holding him at arm's length as she turns him to get a better look. "You're like the cat in the grey flannel suit."

She notices a little silver tag hanging from a collar and sits him back down so she can read it. "'Dapper Dan.' So that's your name." The little cat purrs and trills softly in reply. Maggie turns the tag over to see if there is an address for the owner, but the back side is blank.

"Well, there can't be too many places to look in this little town. You can stay with me tonight and we'll find your owner tomorrow after the storm passes." She reaches out to pet his head and he leans into her hand, purring and rubbing his head against it.

"What a little sweetie you are," Maggie says with a little chuckle. "I bet you'd like some warm milk."

Maggie walks over to the fridge as the cat jumps down off the table to follow her. She opens the door and takes out the half-and-half. She then walks over to the stove and turns one of the burners on low. She takes a small sauce pan from the drying rack next to the sink and places it on the burner where she pours a little of the cream in to warm. She looks in the cupboard and finds a little ceramic bowl, then looks down at the cat, sitting by her feet as he looks up at her to watch her every move.

"Oh, you're gonna love this," she says as she checks the pan. After a few moments, the first little wisps of steam begin to rise from the cream and she pours it into the bowl, sticking a fingertip in to make sure it's not too hot. She turns the burner off and takes the dish over to the fireplace, with Dan following close at her heals.

Maggie bends down and takes one of the newspapers and lays it on the wooden floor. She sets the bowl on the paper and the little cat instantly begins lapping it up, purring contently. Maggie sits on the floor next to him, petting him in long, slow strokes from his head down the length of his back.

"There you go little Danny. This'll warm you up."

The cat continues to purr and drink in the warm glow of the fire. Maggie feels comforted at having the presence of a companion, even if it is just a little cat. She once again begins to feel calm contentment as she listens to the soft purring along with the warm crackling of the fire. The sounds of the raging storm seem to dissolve slightly into the background.

As she continues to pet the little cat, her gaze transitions to the paper that the bowl is sitting on. She notices the headline, "Another Missing Person in Sandy Hollow." The site of the bold words causes her stomach to tighten. She reaches over and moves the bowl off the paper and onto the hardwood as the cat moves with it, continuing to drink. Maggie holds the paper in her hands and finds herself staring at a photo that causes her blood to run cold. Beneath the headline is a picture of a young, blond girl that looks remarkably similar to her. Her hands start to tremble as she begins reading the article.

"State police are investigating the disappearance of 18-year-old Rachel Owens. She was last seen in the town of Sandy Hollow while on her way to Pine Lodge Ski Resort. Authorities are reluctant to comment on the disappearance as it is part of an ongoing investigation. This is not the first missing persons case to be associated with the small town. Over the last two decades there have been" The article abruptly stops with the words, "continued on page 5" below it. Maggie frantically searches through the papers, searching for page 5 but there doesn't seem to be one. She crawls over to the stack of papers next to the kindling box and flips through a few of them and realizes that it must have been one of the papers she used to start the fire.

Maggie slumps back to a sitting position on the floor looking at the picture of the girl. She looks at the date at the top of the page and sees that it is about two years old. Her mind races, thinking about what the old woman had said in the diner and what Brian had told her on the drive up to the cabin. *How many girls have gone missing? Did they all look like me? Why?* The questions begin tumbling around in her mind.

Maggie looks at the cat, who now sits next to the dish, happily cleaning his fur, having finished about two thirds of the warm cream. A strong gust of wind causes the cabin to shutter again and drives some large rain drops against the windows. The lights flicker for a moment. Maggie stands to her feet and makes her way to the small half-bathroom at the back of the stairs to splash some water on her face. She walks through the door and flips the light switch. Suddenly the entire cabin is plunged into darkness. Maggie turns and looks into the living room that is now bathed in ominous looking shadows that dance along the walls, cast by the flickering flames of the fireplace. Dan the cat rests on the floor next to the fireplace, his paws neatly tucked beneath his body and his tail wrapped tight against one side. He looks at her with sleepy eyes, unbothered by the sudden lack of light.

Maggie walks to the middle of the room and stands in silence for a moment, trying to decide if it is just the storm that knocked out the power, or if the breaker was somehow tripped when she flipped the switch. She tries to think where the breaker box is and thinks she remembers it being attached to a small shed just outside the kitchen door. She makes her way over to the door and looks out the window to see the little shed. Sure enough, there is a box attached to the side and a light shining down from the roof above.

"Now why is that light on," she asks aloud, straining to see through the rain. "If the outside lights are on, but the house lights are off, it must be a breaker."

Maggie dreads the idea of going out into the storm to check the box, but decides she should, as she doesn't know how long she'll be alone at the cabin. She walks over to put her shoes and coat back on, flipping the hood up over her head. She looks at the cat, still lying on the floor by the fire.

"I don't suppose you'd like to go out there to check the box," she says to him. His only response is a long, sleepy blink of the eyes.

Maggie walks back over to the kitchen door and looks at the shed through the window. She unlocks and opens the door to a blast of cold wind and rain and lunges outside, closing it behind her. She quickly makes her way down the steps and runs over to the box. The overhang of the roof gives a little shelter from the rain as she opens the door to the box, revealing the row of breaker switches inside. She can't make out the faded labels next to the switches, but sees an orange-colored indicator next to one of them. She flips the heavy switch off and on again and turns to see the lamp light shining through the kitchen window.

Maggie shuts the door to the box and makes her way back to the cabin and up the steps. She enters the kitchen door, closing and locking it behind her, standing on the mat as she shakes the water from her coat and wipes the mud from her feet. She takes her coat off and walks over to hang it up again on the hook by the front door. As she does, she notices something on the floor. She looks closer to see muddy footprints. She puts her foot next to it, confirming that it is larger than hers and obviously a boot tread pattern, definitely not made by her tennis shoes.

A bump causes Maggie to spin around and look to the top of the stairs. Her heart leaps into her throat as she freezes to listen to the creaking floorboards and sounds of footsteps upstairs. She tries to breath, but can't as the terrible reality hits her like a punch in the gut... *Someone's inside the cabin!*

Chapter 5

The Storm

Unable to move, Maggie's heart races as she tries to decide what she should do. She stands there, looking up the stairs for what feels like an eternity as her mind tries to reason through a fight or flight reaction. She knows that someone is inside, but she doesn't know who or why, though with recent events, it doesn't take too much imagination to hazard a guess as to the why. Maggie decides that whoever this person is, she can be sure they have hostile intentions.

Run! The thought leaps to the front of her mind. *But where,* she thinks. She doesn't know the woods, and with the storm and dark of night, she wouldn't know where to go. Her next thought is to fight, but without knowing what she would be up against, her self-doubt quickly overwhelms her.

The upstairs floorboards creak beneath the footsteps of the intruder and it sounds like they are making their way to the top of the stairs. Maggie realizes she must hide and quickly. An idea suddenly pops into her head. *If I leave the front door open and hide inside the cabin, maybe they'll think I ran off into the woods!* The sound approaches the top of the stairs, prompting Maggie to act. She quickly turns the knob and opens the front door, which flings wide with a gust of wind as she runs through the living room, turning the corner at the back of the staircase, crouching down to hide at the bathroom door opening behind them.

At the same moment, unseen by her, a shadowy figure appears atop the staircase, pausing to see the open door below. Maggie can hear the intruder slowly make their way down the stairs, each step causing a feeling of terrible anticipation to well up inside her. As they approach the bottom, Maggie's mind spins with different scenarios and possible outcomes as she tries to plan her next move. *If they go outside, perhaps I can make it to the door and lock them out. But then what? What if they break back in? Are the phone lines still down? Uncle Jake's a hunter, so where does he keep his guns?*

She can hear them slowly walking across the floor to the open, front door and she readies herself. The footsteps stop, and Maggie tries to force herself to peak around the corner, but her fear won't seem to let her. She listens, straining to hear, but can only make out the sound of the storm. She finally manages to position herself so that she can look with her right eye and sees a figure in a yellow, hooded raincoat standing in the doorway looking out. She quickly slinks back to her original hiding position with a gasp and tenses every muscle, trying not to let her fear overwhelm her.

Maggie waits an agonizing amount of time for the intruder to make the next move. *Please, just go out,* she thinks. She wonders if she should try looking again but stays put. Finally, she hears the door shut. *Did they leave,* she wonders. Her curiosity is only met with silence. *Are they still inside? Should I look?*

She hears the creak of a floorboard and holds her breath. Silence again. She waits and hears another creak. *I think they're still inside!* The sound of her own heartbeat pounds in her ears so loudly, she is sure the intruder can hear it. She then feels a burning sensation in her lungs and realizes she is holding her breath. As slowly and quietly as she can, Maggie breaths out. She tightly closes her eyes as she carefully takes another breath in, trying to do so quietly, but the sound, to her, is beyond loud. She holds her breath again, the blood still pounding in her ears, as she strains to listen for the intruder. She hears nothing.

Alright, it's time to look again, she thinks. Carefully and at a pace that would frustrate a sloth, Maggie leans out to take a look. As she does, she begins to see the living room, then her gaze comes to the cat, now sitting up in his spot near the fireplace, his eyes wide as he stares at Maggie. As she continues around the corner, she can see the rest of the empty room and begins to feel a sense of relief when, at the end of her visual sweep, her sight falls on the hooded figure standing just inches from her. Before she can react, she is grabbed by both arms and lifted to her feet.

"No! Let me go," she cries as she struggles and manages to pull free. She falls backward with the force of her movement, slamming against the wall and in one adrenaline assisted thrust, pushes herself off the wall and past her attacker as she desperately makes her way toward the front door.

Maggie's attacker chases after her. Just as she reaches the door and starts to open it, the intruder throws their weight against it, slamming it shut as they once again grab and attempt to restrain her. Maggie manages to jerk free once again and slips on the wet floor, falling into the table and chairs in the kitchen. She quickly scrambles across the floor like a frightened animal, making her way to the counter along the wall and reaches to pull herself up. As she does, she notices the wooden block with the kitchen knives that sits near the back of the counter and reaches for the biggest handle. She pulls the large knife from the block just as the attacker reaches her and with all the strength she can manage, in a swift, arching motion, she slashes at her hooded foe, slicing through the thick rubber sleeve on their left arm, cutting through the flesh, down to the bone.

The attacker stumbles backwards, cradling their wounded limb with their other hand, giving Maggie a brief opportunity to escape. She turns and reaches for the kitchen door, twisting the knob while simultaneously pulling, but it doesn't open. *Locked!* She quickly fumbles with the little lock on the knob, finally managing to turn it. She starts to open the door when she is grabbed from behind by the hair and her head is shoved into the door, slamming it closed with the force of the blow. The room begins to spin, and she finds herself in a state of confused panic as she is dragged over to the pantry where the attacker lifts the trap door on the floor and pushes Maggie toward it, sending her tumbling down into the darkness.

Maggie hits the ground with a thud, landing on her back which knocks the wind out of her. As she lies there looking up at the square opening, she sees the intruder slam the door closed, plunging her into total darkness. Maggie's head reels from the blow she received, and she rolls on the floor, gasping and struggling to catch her breath. She feels as though she is slipping in and out of consciousness, but can hear some commotion up above. In her stuporous state, she thinks that her antagonist must be looking for a first aid kit, or something to treat their wound.

Everything goes quiet for a moment and then comes back. *I must have lost consciousness,* Maggie thinks to herself. She can hear the footsteps up above again and then all goes silent again. The sound of a cabinet slamming jars her back. *I have to stay awake!* Her head pounds and her chest aches from the fall. *I have to find a way out!*

Maggie feels around in the darkness and finds the ladder which she uses to pull herself up. She stands there for a moment wondering if she should try to climb up and get out, but the heavy footsteps above cause her to hesitate. Maggie stumbles a bit in the darkness and feels something lightly brush her face. She instinctually swipes at it with her hand and realizes it is a pull chain for a light. She pulls it, squinting at the sudden burst of illumination, and is surprised to see a well-organized storage space lined with shelves and plastic containers. Her gaze falls to the far side of the room where she sees some concrete steps leading up to a pair of angled cellar doors that open to the outside.

"Oh, thank God," Maggie gasps with excitement.

She quickly makes her way over to the steps, turns the handle and flings the heavy doors open. The wind and rain hit her, though not quite as hard as before, and she finds the cold burst provides a much welcome feeling of rejuvenation and freedom. As she steps up onto the muddy ground and looks around to get her bearings, she realizes she can now see in the soft twilight of the early morning and realizes she must have been unconscious longer than she thought.

She sees the path at the front of the cabin that leads down the hill toward town and takes off running as fast as she can, forgetting the pain and discomfort of her injuries. As she passes the front porch, she thinks she hears the front door open, but she doesn't look back, instead pushing herself to run even harder as she imagines her track coach's voice telling her to keep going, to do better, to fight through the desire to quit.

"When you feel you can't take another step, you run one more step!" The words resound in her head as her training kicks in and her breathing and running fall into rhythm. She sees the fallen tree up ahead, and pushes toward it, hurdling over the lower part with perfect form, splashing into the mud and water as she lands and keeps running.

In the distance, Maggie thinks she hears a motor, like an ATV. She continues to run, now feeling the burning in her chest and an ache in her side.

"One more step! One more step!" She repeats the command again and again as she runs.

The path steepens downward and Maggie realizes she must be getting close to town. She loses her footing on the slippery grade, sliding a few feet but recovers and continues running. Finally, she reaches the bottom and her feet hit the asphalt of the town's main street. The buildings all look dark and deserted as she runs down the street calling for help.

"Help! Please, somebody help me!"

Her cries go unanswered. She sees the sheriff station and runs to open the door, but finds it to be locked. The tears begin running down her cheeks and a lump rises in her throat as she pounds on the door pleading for someone to open it.

"Please! Somebody please let me in! I need help!"

Maggie notices a small sign hanging in the window that reads, "out of the office. Be back soon." She feels her heart sink as she turns to survey the quiet town, wiping her eyes as she does. Just then, a light goes on in one of the upstairs windows above Molly's.

"Oh! Oh, please," she cries as she rushes over and begins pounding on the door while trying to turn the locked knob. "Please, Molly! Help me!"

Maggie keeps pounding and yelling until she sees a light turn on in the back of the diner and then continues even more frantically. She sees Molly appear from the back, wrapped in a light, pink bathrobe as she hurries to open the door. The door flings wide as Maggie falls into Molly's arms, exhausted and sobbing.

"Gracious me, child," Molly exclaims. "What on earth happened?"

Maggie tries to explain, but can only manage to sob, "He's trying to kill me! He's trying to kill me!"

"Who is, dear," Molly asks. "Who's trying to kill you?"

"I don't know! I don't know, but he's trying to kill me!"

Molly shuts the door as she ushers Maggie to a chair next to the fireplace, where the last dying embers softly smolder from last night. "Here, you sit yourself right here," she says as she reaches over and tosses a log onto the embers. "Oh, you poor thing. You're soaked to the bone," she says as she peels Maggie's outer shirt off. She hurries around the corner and returns with a blanket, wrapping it around Maggie's shoulders.

"Now you just sit right here and get warm while I go make you a cup of hot chocolate."

Maggie sits there shivering and holding the blanket tight as Molly disappears into the kitchen. Maggie can hear her rattling things around as she just stares, blankly at the floor. The log in the fireplace begins to burn slightly and the soft warmth and smell of smoke brings her back into the moment. She looks around at the empty diner and stands to her feet as she slowly walks toward the direction of the kitchen.

Maggie stops at the counter, reaching out to steady herself. The night's ordeal has taken its toll and she feels her exhaustion taking over. Her gaze shifts toward the back door where she notices a yellow raincoat hanging on a stand above a pair of boots. She shivers as she notices the cut in the sleeve and the water dripping to the muddy pool on the floor.

Maggie's heart rate increases along with her breathing as she stands paralyzed. Molly reappears from the kitchen with a steaming mug.

"Oh, sweetie, you should be sitting down," Molly says, holding the cup out to her.

Maggie backs away, keeping her eyes on Molly. Molly hesitates, looking confused before holding the cup out to her again.

"Here, I've made you some hot chocolate."

Maggie backs away again, looking at the cup being offered to her. She notices a white bandage wrapped around Molly's arm.

"What happened to your arm," Maggie asks.

"Oh, that? I scraped it on the corner of the grill last night," Molly says with a soft chuckle. "Now here, child, drink this."

"I thought your cook was cleaning the grill last night," Maggie says, still backing away, cautiously.

Suddenly Molly stops and the kind, motherly expression dissolves from her face. Her eyes now look cold and dark, her face stern.

"I really think you should drink this," she says taking another step towards Maggie. "It's rude not to accept a person's help."

"Why, Molly," Maggie asks. "Why is it so important that I drink the hot chocolate?"

"Just drink it!" The screamed command surprises Maggie, causing her to gasp and jump slightly. Molly still holds the cup out, her eyes now wild with anger. Maggie suddenly feels a surge of anger too.

"Drink it yourself you psychopath," she says. She then lunges forward and shoves Molly backwards, sending the cup and its contents flying and Molly stumbling to the floor. Maggie rushes through the door and into the street outside.

The storm has calmed, but the rain falls steady. Maggie sees the Sheriff's car coming up the street toward her and runs to it, waving her arms.

"Stop! Stop, please," she yells.

The car quickly stops, and the red and blue lights begin to flash. Maggie hurries around to the driver's door, which flings open and the sheriff steps out looking somewhat confused.

"Alright, Miss. Just slow down," he begins as Maggie starts talking faster than he can process. "Calm down. What's wrong?"

Before Maggie can answer, Molly bursts through the diner door holding a shotgun. The sheriff steps in front of Maggie, towards Molly, the look of concerned confusion intensified upon his brow.

"Molly? What in tarnation you doin' with that shotgun," he yells.

Molly raises the weapon and takes aim, causing the sheriff to instinctively reach for his gun. He holds his left hand toward her, with his right hand on the handle of the pistol, protectively keeping his large frame between her and Maggie.

"Molly, I think you'd better fill me in on what's goin' on here!"

"Get out of the way, Joe," she yells.

"I can't do that Molly," he replies. "Now why don't you just lower that shotgun, so we can talk."

"I said move!" Molly pumps the shotgun as she screams the command, ejecting a shell that was already loaded, causing another to load into the chamber.

The sheriff draws his weapon and points it at Molly.

"Molly! Don't make me have to do something I'm gonna regret here. You're puttin' me in a bad spot."

Molly begins to tremble as she holds the weapon on them. Her face is a jumble of emotion; mostly hate and anger, with a wave of sadness as she starts crying.

"Why don't you tell me why you're trying to harm this girl," the sheriff says, keeping his gun trained on her.

The barrel of the shotgun starts to lower as Molly sobs her reply.

"Because she killed my Danny."

A look of confusion overtakes the sheriff.

"What!?!"

"My Danny's dead! He's dead and it's all her fault," she says, sobbing even harder as the barrel dips a little lower.

"Molly, this girl wasn't even born when Danny died!"

"Don't say that," Molly screams, raising the shotgun again, causing the sheriff to tense as he aims his pistol and Maggie to cling tighter to the back of his shirt as she peers around his large arm. "She killed him! He had his whole life ahead of him before she came along!"

"Molly that's crazy! That was nearly twenty years ago. That was a different girl entirely."

"Don't lie for her, Joe!"

Another sheriff's car pulls up behind Molly and a confused deputy steps out drawing his pistol, looking to Joe to tell him what to do. Joe just puts his hand out toward him, indicating that he's handling it and the deputy shouldn't take any action yet. Molly begins sobbing even harder and lets the barrel of the shotgun fall to the ground with a metallic clink. Her shoulders slump as she talks through the tears.

"He was such a good boy. My baby boy. Why did she have to come along, filling his head with nonsense, getting him all confused. He'd still be here, Joe. He'd still be alive. Don't you see that?"

"I don't know, Molly. I don't know. Why don't you put that gun down and we can talk about it? We'll see if we can get this all straightened out."

She lets out a mournful cry as she lets the shotgun slip from her fingers to the ground. The deputy behind her quickly steps forward and grabs her arm, holstering his weapon so he can cuff her. Joe holsters his gun too as he turns to see Maggie standing there in a state of wide-eyed shock. He places a hand on her shoulder.

"You alright little miss?"

"I don't understand," she replies. "What happened? I don't understand what just happened."

"Well, I'm not really sure myself darlin'," he replies, looking over to see the deputy leading Molly to the jail. "We'll get it straightened out though and hopefully get her the help she needs."

Maggie suddenly becomes overwhelmed with emotion and collapses onto the sheriff's chest as she cries. He wraps his big bear-like arms around her as he tries to calm and reassure her.

"Hey now little lady. It's okay. You're alright." He places his big finger under her chin, lifting it up so her eyes meet his own as he smiles kindly at her. "See? You're safe now."

Maggie nods and wipes her eyes, feeling a little better.

"Thank you," she says, gathering her composure.

"My pleasure, Miss," he replies. "Now, let's get in out of the rain and see if we can put a call in to your dad and uncle."

He puts his arm around Maggie's shoulder and slowly walks her to the office door.

"I think we have some hot chocolate mix. Would you like some hot chocolate?"

"No, thank you," Maggie replies, softly as they enter the office and the sheriff closes the door behind them.

ABOUT THE AUTHOR

J.S. Cuncle is an American Author from the beautiful state of Idaho. A graduate from Boise State University, he holds a Bachelor of Business Administration in both General Business Management and Marketing with a minor in Visual Art and is also a certified teacher working in the Boise School District. An artist at heart, J.S. enjoys working in many various art forms, including but not limited to photography, painting, graphic design, and now writing. Encouraged by positive feedback, J.S. decided to test the writing waters by entering some of his work into contests. He took second place in his very first contest and placed in the top three, including a few first-place entries, in several others. He has now decided to take the next step and publish his first short story, Sandy Hollow, and plans to publish more of his books in the future.